MOON'S
Cloud Blanket

MOON'S
Cloud Blanket

Rose Anne St. Romain

**Illustrated by
Joan C. Waites**

PELICAN PUBLISHING COMPANY
Gretna 2003

To my sweet Moma and my good Daddy

Special thanks to Gray Hawk, my Houma-Choctaw friend,
for helping me craft this story from his memories of
a tale told to him by the elders
—R. A. S. R.

The word "Pelican" and the depiction of a pelican are trademarks
of Pelican Publishing Company, Inc., and are registered
in the U.S. Patent and Trademark Office.

Library of Congress Cataloging-in-Publication Data

St. Romain, Rose Anne.
  Moon's cloud blanket / Rose Anne St. Romain ; illustrated by Joan C. Waites.
    p. cm.
Summary: In this retelling of a Native American tale, the Moon weaves a blanket of clouds around a mother and her children who are freezing atop a cypress tree, having sought shelter from a flood.
  ISBN 1-56554-922-8 (hardcover)
  1. Indians of North America—Louisiana—Folklore. 2. Spanish moss—Folklore. 3. Legends—Louisiana. [1. Indians of North America—Louisiana—Folklore. 2. Spanish moss—Folklore. 3. Folklore—Louisiana.] I. Waites, Joan C., ill. II. Title.
  E78.L8 S8 2002
  398.2'089'97—dc21

                                        2002009501

Printed in China
Published by Pelican Publishing Company, Inc.
1000 Burmaster Street, Gretna, Louisiana 70053

MOON'S CLOUD BLANKET

Long ago, in South Louisiana, a woman was working in her garden. Nearby her little boy practiced with his blow-gun while her little girl counted wildflowers. It began to rain so hard that the woman could not see her hoe.

The woman and her children sought shelter in their palmetto hut and waited for the rain to stop. But the rain would not stop. It rained and rained until the bayous overflowed. It rained and rained until the rivers overflowed.

It rained and rained until the water found its way into the palmetto hut. When the water reached her ankles, the woman became concerned. For still the rain came down and still the water rose.

When it reached her knees, she became afraid. For still the rain came down and still the water rose. And when it reached her waist, she became alarmed. For still the rain came down and still the water rose.

The woman knew that she and her children must find higher ground or else they would surely drown. Holding her two children tightly, one under each arm, the woman stepped out of her palmetto hut and into the storm.

The wind whipped her hair about while the rain pelted her face. Frantically, the woman looked around for higher ground. But in South Louisiana, there is no higher ground. The land lies flat all the way to the Gulf of Mexico.

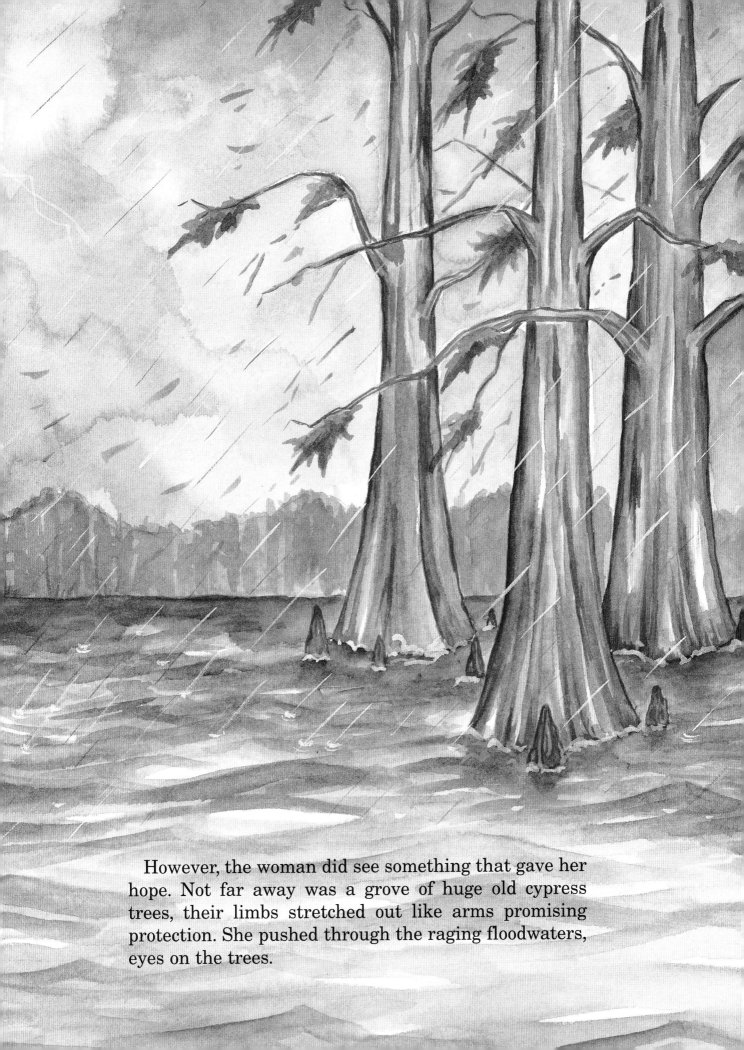

However, the woman did see something that gave her hope. Not far away was a grove of huge old cypress trees, their limbs stretched out like arms promising protection. She pushed through the raging floodwaters, eyes on the trees.

All around the woman the water swirled and churned. Lightning split the sky while thunder crashed and rolled. The wind was so strong that it snapped huge limbs off the trees as if they were mere twigs.

A whirlpool pulled her under and she struggled to find her footing, still holding her children tightly. Gasping and sputtering, she fought the current, pushing on toward the trees. And still the rain came down and still the water rose.

Reaching a cypress, she lifted her children and herself into the tree. They had to climb to the highest branches. From their perch they could see for miles and miles around. All they could see was water, water, everywhere.

And still the rain came down and still the water rose. The wind howled. The rain pounded. The children huddled close to their mother. The woman rocked them gently, grateful for their warmth.

Finally, at sunset, the rain stopped. But the wind still shrieked and wailed and moaned and chilled them to the bone. The children's teeth chattered behind bluish lips. Now the woman was afraid they would freeze this night.

Her hope was renewed when Moon came out, pale and round. The woman told Moon of her fears and asked for help in keeping her children warm. She begged Moon to save them from death, then fell asleep exhausted.

They say that Moon heard the woman's plea. Moon
spoke to Stars. Stars spoke to Clouds. Clouds spoke to
Wind. And Wind stopped.

They say that Moon reached up, pulled down the tattered shreds of gray clouds still trailing across the heavens, and wove them together. All night long, Moon wove and wove and wove.

In the morning, the little boy was the first one to awaken. He cried out to his mother: What was this covering them? When the woman opened her eyes she saw why her child was frightened.

They were covered by a strange blanket woven from grayish grass all wispy and tattered like the last clouds of a storm. The woman understood. She understood that Moon had woven a blanket for them from Clouds.

The woman told her children that it was Moon's Cloud Blanket that had kept them warm and safe. She and her children thanked Moon for the gift. They stayed nestled under Moon's Cloud Blanket for many days and nights.

Finally, when the floodwaters receded, the woman and her children could leave the tree. The woman tried to take the Cloud Blanket with her. But anything woven from Clouds is very fragile, and Moon's Cloud Blanket tore.

The woman was gifted with only a handful. She did not take more than the tree gave her. She thanked the tree for its protection and went on her way with her children.

But the Cloud Blanket? It was alive. It was alive! It grew and spread all through that first tree. Other trees whose branches entwined with that first one soon had Cloud Blanket growing along their limbs.

Little birds came from far away and took wisps of
Cloud Blanket to keep their own babies' beds
warm. And in this way, they say, Moon's Cloud
Blanket was spread to many, many trees in
Louisiana and the South.

And to this day, as we travel the highways and byways and bayous of Louisiana, we can see Moon's Cloud Blanket trailing elegantly from trees. But we no longer call it Moon's Cloud Blanket.

We call it Spanish moss.

AUTHOR'S NOTE

For generations, Spanish moss has helped provide for my family. When my great-grandparents, grandparents, and parents were children, they picked moss from the trees in Plaucheville, Louisiana to stuff their handmade mattresses or to sell for fifty cents per one hundred pounds of moss. When I was a child, my father took his eight children for rides in the woods in his old Jeep to gather moss to camouflage duck-hunting blinds. Mom's wild-duck gumbo was a winter food staple in our big family, thanks to Spanish moss.

When I first encountered this story in 1988, I was drawn to the theme of the woman's dependency on the natural world even as it threatened to destroy her. My ancestors, too, lived in the balance of nature's scales. —R. A. S. R.